From Pizza to Pisa

By Alicia Klepeis

Illustrated by Simon Abbott

www.rourkeeducationalmedia.com

Edited by: Keli Sipperley
Cover and Interior layout by: Renee Brady
Cover and Interior Illustrations by: Simon Abbott

Library of Congress PCN Data

From Pizza to Pisa / Alicia Klepeis
(Rourke's World Adventure Chapter Books)
ISBN (hard cover)(alk. paper) 978-1-63430-399-6
ISBN (soft cover) 978-1-63430-499-3
ISBN (e-Book) 978-1-63430-593-8
Library of Congress Control Number: 2015933799

Printed in the United States of America,
North Mankato, Minnesota

Dear Parents and Teachers:

Rourke's Adventure Chapter Books engage readers immediately by grabbing their attention with exciting plots and adventurous characters.

Our Adventure Chapter Books offer longer, more complex sentences and chapters. With minimal illustrations, readers must rely on the descriptive text to understand the setting, characters, and plot of the book. Each book contains several detailed episodes all centered on a single plot that will challenge the reader.

Each adventure book dives into a country. Readers are not only invited to tag along for the adventure but will encounter the most memorable monuments and places, culture, and history. As the characters venture throughout the country, they address topics of family, friendship, and growing up in a way that the reader can relate to.

Whether readers are reading the books independently or you are reading with them, engaging with them after they have read the book is still important. We've included several activities at the end of each book to make this both fun and educational.

Are you ready for this adventure?

Enjoy,
Rourke Educational Media

Table of Contents

A Mysterious Phone Call

"You're up next, Ollie. Your category is Revolting. Disgusting. Repulsive. Hideous." Anara was setting up her younger brother Oliver for the next round of their favorite board game, Apples to Apples.

"Quite the appropriate category for a seven-year-old boy, don't you think?" quipped Anara's twin, Samal. The three Nylund kids were spending the weekend at their dad's place in Brooklyn. It was just before Thanksgiving break.

"Be quiet, you guys. Your categories should have been Mean and Grumpy." Oliver was learning to fight back against his sisters' tag team threat.

"Good one, Ollie. You tell 'em!" Dad was impressed. Suddenly, the phone rang. "Could you pick that up, Samal?"

Samal grabbed the phone. She was surprised to hear Mom's voice on the other end. Normally when they spent the weekend at Dad's, they heard nothing from Mom between Friday night drop-off and Sunday night pickup. Samal thought Mom sounded rather mysterious. Not like her usual self.

Seeing the funny look on her sister's face, Anara mouthed, "Who is it?"

Sam pointed at the phone and mouthed back, "Mom." With their furrowed brows, the 10-year-old identical twins really looked the same–both expression-wise and with their flushed cheeks and frizzy blonde hair.

Ever since they got divorced three years ago, Mom and Dad were polite to each other. But they certainly didn't just call up and chat for no reason. Dad took his cell phone onto the small back patio.

"Where's Dad going?" Ollie wanted to know. "It's freezing out there."

"I guess he doesn't want us to eavesdrop. The walls are pretty thin here," Samal answered.

About 20 minutes later, Dad came back inside with a grin on his face. The kids had been speculating about their parents' conversation. Were they discussing progress reports from school? Plans for Christmas vacation? The girls were dying to know what was going on. Anara couldn't keep quiet/ "What's up? Why did Mom call? We just got here last night."

"We'll talk over dinner," Dad said. "Don't stress. Nothing bad is going on."

Ollie insisted that they finish their game. But the girls were totally distracted, to the point where Ollie won five rounds in a row. Anara crowned him victor with an old plastic fruit wreath. Oliver beamed, though he looked ridiculous.

For dinner, the Nylunds walked to their favorite pizzeria, Grimaldi's, right under the Brooklyn Bridge. Samal thought the restaurant choice was strange since they usually only went there for special occasions.

Once seated, the girls said they couldn't wait any longer for the news. Dad pretended he couldn't hear their request as he glanced at the menu. But Samal noticed that he had crinkly smile lines around his eyes so she knew he was listening.

Finally, he spoke. "Mom called because she was given a work assignment in Italy. The trip will be in

February. If you go, you'd only miss about a week and a half of school. I know your grandma Vovó couldn't make it in October when you guys went to Egypt, but she really wants to come on this trip. For the first part of the trip, Vovó will hang out with you while Mom is working. And I'll come for the last 10 days or so. We can even celebrate Oliver's birthday there!"

The twins and Ollie looked at each. A wide grin spread over each of their faces.

"Are you serious? You never take vacation time, Dad!" Anara said. It was rare for Dad to take time off from his job as a doctor. They hadn't gone on a vacation with him since the divorce.

Something else was perplexing Samal. "Does this mean that you and Mom are getting back together?"

"No, honey. But Mom and I are still friends. Neither of us wants to pass up this opportunity to travel with you guys. Plus, it's rather unusual that I don't have any surgeries scheduled yet for those dates."

Their mother's work for the United Nations Educational, Scientific and Cultural Organization often sent them to fun places. But this trip with Dad and Vovo along would be extra special.

Over garlic knots, margarita pizza, and cannoli, the Nylunds brainstormed about their trip to Italy. After watching a National Geographic special about the sinking city, Anara wanted to see Venice. Samal said she hoped to ride a gondola and eat tons of gelato. Oliver, a history buff, wanted to see some Roman ruins.

Getting ready to go to Italy required some planning. Oliver researched what February's weather would be like in Rome, Venice, and Modena. Since he loved playing with Mom's smartphone, this was no hardship. Ollie reported that Venice and Modena were likely to be in the 40s for most of the trip. Rome was supposed to be a little warmer, in the mid-50s.

The twins made packing lists for themselves and Ollie, skipping the boring stuff like conditioner and soap.

The last few days before the trip were hectic. On the ride home from school one day, Samal had a small meltdown. "Mom, my teachers are being so unfair! I have to take math, science, social studies

Rome Packing List:

- Owl onesie (Samal), Fleecy pajamas (Anara, Ollie)
- Sneakers and hiking boots
- Foldable rain jackets
- Corduroy pants, jeans, and leggings
- T-shirts, plus a few long-sleeved tunics
- Sweater dresses and skirts
- Cape Cod sweatshirts and one fleece per person
- Underwear and socks
- Small backpacks
- Journals
- Activities for plane ride
- Books

- Digital camera
- Pens, colored pencils, markers
- Sketchpad (Anara)
- Stuffed animals (Samal – rainbow chameleon; Anara – elephant; Oliver – buffalo)

and English tests all before we leave. Everyone else gets to take them next week. I haven't even learned all the material yet!"

Mom sighed. "I know it's a bummer now but when you're having adventures all over Italy, you'll think it was worth it."

The twins nodded. At least their teachers didn't give them any homework over the break. Instead they just asked Samal and Anara to keep journals while they were in Italy.

******

With bags packed and tests taken, it was nearly time to leave. But when Ollie flipped on the Weather Channel, the meteorologists were predicting a serious ice storm for New York.

Would their trip be canceled?

A Roman Cat-astrophe

When the kids woke up on departure day, the power lines outside of their apartment window glistened. Tree branches, wires, and even the sidewalks were coated in a thick, shiny layer of ice. Anara looked at the airline website to check their flight. Many of the morning flights had already been canceled. Sam said the TV news announced that airport crews were working to de-ice the runways.

Despite the still-messy roads, a taxi came to their apartment to pick them up around dinnertime. After a slight delay at the airport, they boarded the plane.

Everything started out smoothly on the overnight flight to Rome's Leonardo da Vinci International Airport. Then they hit turbulence. Samal refused to take motion sickness medicine before the flight, saying that she only got sick on windy car rides. As their flight hit what the pilot delicately called "rough air," Samal got a serious case of nausea. Ollie, on the other hand, got a case of the giggles as the plane bounced up and down.

"I think I'm gonna be sick," Samal gasped. "Find me one of those air sickness bags – quick!" Anara thrust the bag into her sister's hand just before Samal wretched violently.

"Eew," Ollie scrunched up his nose. "That stinks like smoothie. Gross!"

"You're lucky I'm empty now, Ollie, or I'd barf on you!" Samal wiped her mouth. Her hands shook. And she was not happy with her little brother.

"Now I know I really have earned my nickname the Dramamine Queen. Next flight, I'm taking some."

The turbulence soon settled and Samal returned to her normal shade of pale. Not the pistachio color she's been shortly before. Between the turbulence and cramped quarters, both girls were pretty beat when they arrived in Rome, "the Eternal City," the next afternoon. But Ollie, who'd slept across everyone's laps, was full of energy.

Anara asked, "Can we have some sugar to keep us going? Some of us," she said, glaring at Oliver, "didn't get much sleep."

"Of course. Rules are meant to be broken on vacation," Mom said.

The twins perked up after a soda from a shop at the airport. They hopped into a taxi and made their way to the city center. Ollie noticed that the cabs in Rome weren't yellow like in New York. Instead, they were white with the Roman crest on the door. In his accented English, the driver told them that the initials SPQR on the taxi door stood for Senatus Populusque Romanus, which was Latin for "the Senate and People of Rome."

Samal, an architecture fan, gave their accommodations in Rome her thumbs up seal of approval. She loved their room's tiny balcony with its view of the hotel's courtyard and fountain. The weather was glorious and sunny.

After being cooped up so long, Ollie was restless. "Let's get out of here and get some food. It's so nice out."

But Anara had other plans. "Dude, I feel disgusting. The guy next to me on the plane reeked. I want to take a quick shower."

Samal agreed with her brother, which was a rare occurrence at home. "Seriously? You can't shower later? I'm the one who puked on the flight. Does Princess Anara need to look good for the masses? They can just look at my lovely face and hair to see what beauty is."

Anara and Samal regularly taunted each other about their looks. But Samal was irritated with Anara's dramas – and her vanity – at the moment.

Anara won that round, though. After a quick shower, the Nylunds wandered down the Via Condotti, a window-shopper's dream. Anara pointed out all the stylish women coming out of designer stores like Giorgio Armani and Valentino. She gushed over the colorful jewels in the Bulgari store window. Mom laughed. "Anara, I don't know what kind of career you're planning on, but you have very expensive tastes. The Via Condotti is probably the ritziest shopping street in all of Rome. It's the Roman version of Fifth Avenue in New York. But the store windows are beautiful."

Oliver was not impressed with the people-watching and slow walking. "Is there anywhere to eat here? I'm starving!"

Samal raised her voice. "Chill out, Ollie! I'm hungry too. Mom just wanted to show us Rome's glamorous side."

They soon arrived at a restaurant with outdoor tables. "Can you believe we're going to eat our first meal in Rome outside? This is awesome!"

They ordered bruschetta and artichokes served with oil, garlic, and mint as appetizers. For their main courses, the kids voted on gnocchi, little dumplings made of semolina flour and served with tomato sauce, and spaghetti alle vongole, a pasta dish with baby clams and tomatoes. After airplane food and long stretches between meals, they ate like bears waking up from hibernation.

Afterward, the twins wanted to go for a walk. Anara knew if they went back to the room she'd fall asleep right away. And with a belly full of Coke, Oliver was rearin' to go. Samal didn't really care what they did so long as she got gelato before bed.

As they wandered through the streets, they stopped in at the Sacro Cuore di Gesú al Castro Pretorio, a 19th century Catholic church. Samal asked for ten minutes to make a quick sketch of the building. Ollie was happy to run around while she drew. They also stopped briefly at the Sapienza University of Rome. Flipping through their guidebook, Anara discovered that the university was founded in 1303. They did a quick walk-through of campus with its old, columned buildings. Students raced from one building to another. Others played Frisbee in a courtyard.

Ollie asked, “Do you think I can join in their Frisbee game? This place is kind of boring.”

“They don’t want snotty-nosed little kids playing,” Anara said.

“You’re mean,” Ollie told her. Mom gave Anara a death-ray stare that told her to be quiet –fast. Samal entertained herself by using Mom’s phone to see if there was a gelato place nearby.

Sam’s research paid off. Just a few minutes away was the ultimate gelato paradise: Fatamorgana Gelato. The shop specialized in all-natural Italian ice creams and sorbets. Oliver was the first to select his two scoops: white chocolate and apricot. Anara couldn’t resist roasted almond and tangerine. Samal wanted to try tiramisu and redcurrant. They

devoured their bedtime snacks in absolute silence.

Just before everyone crashed for the night, Mom said, “I have a little card for each of you to put in your jacket pocket or backpack whenever we leave the hotel. It has UNESCO office’s number and our hotel’s address on it. If we ever get separated, you could show this to a policeman or shop owner. I’m also giving each of you some euros to keep in case of emergency. Got it?”

Samal rolled her eyes and asked, “Is needing to try a new flavor of gelato an emergency worthy of these euros?”

“Ha! You’re a funny girl, Sam.” She rumpled Samal’s crazy hair. “But you do make me laugh. Now let’s get some shut-eye.”

******

The next day–their only full day together–Mom let the kids choose their destinations. Her only restriction: There had to be some time outdoors. The kids scoured their various guidebooks to see what sounded cool.

Ollie’s choice, the Palatine, started the day. The open-air museum was once home to Roman emperors. Oliver loved the frescoes in the House of Augustus. He imagined what it would have been like to walk along the grounds when everything was new.

Anara asked to take a tour of the Said Vintage Chocolate Factory. She thought the factory's old-fashioned machines were neat. Everyone loved the numerous free samples and the heavenly smell in the building.

Before they'd even set food on Italian soil, Samal had her heart set on visiting the Largo di Torre Argentina Cat Sanctuary. Her friends called her "the future crazy cat lady" because she planned to have as many cats as she could when she grew up. The sanctuary was located at the site of Julius Caesar's assassination in 44 BCE. An underground storage shed once used by archaeologists housed blind and disabled kitties. About 200 furry felines lived amid the ancient ruins.

And thanks to all those cats, by the time they left the sanctuary, Anara was sneezing up a storm.

"Your eyes are red. You look like an alien," Ollie said. "What's wrong with you?"

"I don't know," Anara snapped. "My eyes are SO

itchy. It's driving me crazy!"

Mom asked her, "Have you been picking up and patting a lot of cats, Anara? You look like you're having an allergic reaction to them."

"You never told me I was allergic to cats, Mom! Yes, I picked up lots of them. They were so cute! What am I supposed to do now?" Anara was upset. She was also super-uncomfortable.

After asking the volunteers at the cat sanctuary for advice, they headed to a local medical clinic about ten minutes away. By the time they got there, Anara had hives on her face and chest. She also had several bright red patches on her arms. She was wheezing slightly and sneezing constantly.

Using an Italian phrasebook to translate, Mom tried to explain what happened. The nurse gave Anara a shot and within about fifteen minutes, her symptoms started to calm down. The doctor also gave her a prescription so she could calm any allergic symptoms until she got back to New York.

"Why do these things always happen to me?" Anara moaned.

"Because you're a drama magnet," Samal said.

Ollie giggled. Anara sighed heavily, narrowed her eyes, and shook her head. Mom winked at Samal–when Anara wasn't looking, of course.

Gardens and Gladiator School

Oliver tiptoed out of bed before the girls were awake. He was about to set up a little toy soldier game on the rug when he came across their grandmother Vovó sleeping on the pullout couch. Her evening flight from Helsinki hadn't arrived in Rome until nearly midnight. Mom, who'd just gotten out of the shower, whispered to Ollie to let everyone snooze a little longer.

Within an hour, everyone was awake. The kids all gave big hugs to Vovó. They had lots of news to share, especially about the cat crisis.

"Can we do something outdoorsy today, Vovó?" Ollie asked. "I know when we get home we won't be able to play outside much."

"You and I are on the same page, little man. I know just the place we should go. Ukki and I went there on our honeymoon many years ago." Ukki was

Vovó's husband. He passed away before Ollie was born.

"Where is it?" Samal asked.

"You, m'lady, will have to be in suspense just a little longer." She had a funny grin on her face.

"So that's where Dad gets his love of surprises," Samal said.

"Guilty as charged," Vovó said, smiling.

A little while later, they wandered along the Via Vittorio Veneto to get to their mystery destination. They soon arrived at the bike rental kiosk at Borghese Gardens.

"Can we rent that awesome bike that carries multiple people?" Anara asked. "That looks fun."

Ollie read from the sign. "It even has an electric motor that can help pedal when its occupants are tired!"

"Are you guys serious? That thing is huge!," Samal said. "Everyone is going to stare at us. Can't we just rent normal bikes? Or is everyone too lazy to pedal with their own power?"

You're being a party pooper, Sam. This is cool! When are we ever going to find a bike like this again?"

Anara gave her twin a dirty look.

Ollie and Anara said that it was two against one. But in the end, everyone won out. Vovó rented the big bike for the three of them and a foot-powered bicycle for Samal. When Vovó was out of earshot, Anara said, "Because of you, Vovó had to pay for two bikes. I hope your leg muscles ache by the end of the day."

Samal fumed a bit but was glad she could ride as she wanted. She did feel slightly guilty about the extra money but decided she'd offer to pay for her bike rental from her allowance money. By the end of the day, Sam's thigh muscles were sore from all the hills she rode up. Meanwhile, her siblings taunted her as they effortlessly cruised up the hills.

After a full day of exploring the secret gardens, fountains, and many pathways, the group was a bit weary. Heading back toward the hotel, they passed Rome's famous Trevi Fountain. The kids threw a few euro coins in for good luck. Oliver loved the sculpture in the fountain of an unruly seahorse. He wanted to dip his feet in the water but the signs warned against it.

A few blocks from the fountain was an English bookstore. Each of the kids got to choose a new book. Back at the hotel, while Oliver read his new Italian folktales book, the girls had a blast watching Italian commercials on TV.

******

"What are we doing today?" Ollie asked over breakfast the next morning.

"Something for everyone. I've booked you all in for Gladiator School this afternoon." Vovó seemed quite pleased with herself.

"No way! That's awesome!" Ollie was practically hyperventilating. As a lover of all things Roman, he was totally psyched about the day's plan.

"Really, Vovó? Do we have to go?" Samal asked. Anara was thinking the same thing.

"Well, I know Oliver has toy Roman soldiers and lots of books and DVDs at home about the Roman civilization. The reviews on several websites for Gladiator School looked great. There will be plenty of things geared for you girls throughout this trip. I promise."

On the way to the train, Vovó stopped in front

of a store that said Tabaccaio. The shop's sign had a picture of a pipe on it. "Why are we going into a tobacco shop? Have you taken up smoking?" Anara joked.

"Of course not," Vovó giggled. "That's a horrible habit. But here in Italy, the tobacco shops have some of the best assortments of candy and gum. Why don't you each choose one kind of gum and one pack of sweets to save for later? But no American stuff. Only Italian treats."

After the kids made their selections, they headed to Gladiator School. Their instructor, Mario, was tall and muscular. Anara whispered to Samal that she wouldn't want to mess with him.

Their two-hour class started with a gladiator history lesson at the Grupo Storico Romano Museum. All three Nylunds had a blast dressing up. The twins took loads of selfies decked out in tunics, leather sandals, and wooden swords. Mario turned out to be a hilarious teacher. He worked them hard in their exercises, making sure they could jump and move quickly. After their warm-up, Mario also taught them how to duel properly. Samal was a "natural warrior," according to Mario. And Ollie was proud when he received a certificate with his new Gladiator name, Tiberius, at the end of the lesson.

Ollie suggested a picnic dinner in the hotel room that night. The family watched the sun set from their balcony and ate wood-fired pizza from the hotel restaurant. The twins decided to take a bathing suit bubble bath. That was a favorite winter tradition back home whenever someone had a case of the blahs or just wanted to chill out.

Just before bedtime, Anara checked Vovó's phone for the next day's weather. "I think the sunshine is coming to an end, guys. It's not looking great for tomorrow."

Crisis at the Catacombs

"Time for a Plan B," Anara said, pulling the curtains aside the next morning to reveal the downpour. "The idea of sightseeing in the rain all day does not sound appealing."

"Seriously," Samal agreed. "Let's see what's recommended for a rainy day in Rome." While Ollie kept busy reading one of his new gladiator books, the girls flipped through their guidebooks for ideas. "Anara, what do you think about going to the Catacombs? It looks kind of creepy."

"I'm game," Anara answered. "Do you think Ollie will be scared?"

"No, I won't be," Ollie said, tossing a pillow at his sisters.

******

About fifteen people were waiting for the tour to begin when the Nylunds arrived. Their guide,

Violetta, took them down some steps into one of the underground burial chambers known as the Roman Catacombs. She led them through long-forgotten passages and temples hidden beneath Rome's modern piazzas and streets.

Stopping in at the Basilica San Clemente, Violetta told a fascinating story. "It may be hard to believe, folks, but in this beautiful church full of frescos and mosaics, a clergyman had an unusual experience. You see, he heard running water coming from below the basilica. His curiosity got the better of him. So what did he do? He dug his way through the floor tiles of this building. Below ground he discovered what we call today 'the wedding cake.' Basically, it's layers of history piled on top of each other. Let's check out some of the 2,000 year history under this magnificent structure."

The group descended to see a fourth century church, then the second century remains of a temple dedicated to the Roman god Mithras. Finally, about fifty-seven feet below the surface, they came upon an amazingly preserved Roman street from the first century. Oliver and his sisters couldn't believe how much was hidden beneath the Eternal City's streets.

About ten minutes later, as they continued the tour, Samal approached Vovó. "Is Ollie with you?" Vovó looked back at Sam with horror. Where was Oliver? There had been many twists, turns, and mysterious turnoffs since they'd left the basilica. Vovó spoke with Violetta. She was shaking.

The girls started shouting, "Ollie! Where are you, Ollie?" Violetta told the group that they'd need to pause to find Oliver. There were way too many caverns and tunnels for a seven-year-old boy to find his way out on his own. The twins, Vovó, and a dozen strangers started combing the nearest nooks and crannies. Everyone yelled for Oliver.

Without cell phone coverage underground, calling the police was not an option. They were way too far along the tunnels to get above ground quickly. After about thirty minutes, "cuckoo" sounds came from way ahead of them. It was Ollie! Another tour group ahead of theirs had found him in a hidden crypt. Seeing Ollie's ticket stub, the other group leader helped him make his way back in the direction he thought the tour might be headed. Vovó and Violetta thanked everyone for all their help.

With his face a splotchy red mess, Oliver looked very little. He was twirling his hair. After visiting the creepy Bone Chapel, Violetta led the group to the surface. Ollie held tightly to Vovó. "I want to go home," he kept saying. All four of them felt like they'd just gone through some real gladiator battles.

Samal told her brother, "I know you feel like you want to go home, Ollie. But the worst is behind us. It's our last day in Rome. Let's stick close together, okay?" Ollie didn't look convinced but seemed to relax a bit when they sat around a leather booth in a quiet restaurant a little while later.

After some fresh pasta and Parmesan cheese, they walked into the café next door. Anara loved its name, Cristalli di Zucchero, which translated to "sugar crystals." Everyone filled their bellies with steamed milk, miniature pastries, and pretty cakes. Oliver and the girls played some word games at the table.

Just around the corner from their dessert spot was a tram stop. Samal suggested taking a tram ride through the city so they could look out the window and relax. Tram No. 3 passed many Roman landmarks, from ancient walls to aqueducts. By the time they arrived in front of the Roman Colosseum, they'd been on the tram for about an hour. Ollie asked if they could pop out for a bit and see it up close. Since no one was in the mood to take a tour, they bought a self-guided visitor pamphlet. Oliver read some fun facts about the Colosseum to everyone. Then the three of them took turns taking photos with their new digital camera.

"OK, guys, I know it's been a bit of a day. I also know that it's our last day in the Eternal City. Is there anywhere you really want to go that you'd be disappointed to miss?" Vovó rarely shared her own ideas about what she'd like to see, with the exception of sweet shops and bakeries.

Art lover Anara spoke up. "I read about Macro: Museo d'Arte Contemporanea. Do you think we could go, just for like forty-five minutes? I think Sam will dig its architecture. Speaking of digging, there are the remains of an ancient Roman house unearthed during the museum's restoration in the parking lot."

"Sounds great," their grandmother said. "But I'm

splurging on a cab. I think we've had quite enough underground time for a while." She ruffled Ollie's sandy hair and squeezed his hand.

Before they explored the museum, they each bought a tiny sketchpad and a lightweight set of proper artist pencils to share. Ollie and his sisters wandered from gallery to gallery, sketching various things. Samal loved the museum's bathrooms. They had mirrored walls and translucent sinks that flashed different colors as you used them.

Back at the hotel, the kids dispersed to different corners of the room. Samal wrote out some postcards to her friends back home. Anara watched Sesame Street, "Sesamo Apriti," in Italian for laughs. By the end of the hour-long episode, she taught everyone how to count to ten in Italian.

Later they went to a nearby market, where the kids chose fruit, cheese, and bread. On their way back to the hotel, they heard music coming from an old church as they passed by. "Can we go in, just for a minute?" Anara pleaded.

Vovó quipped, "When in Rome!" Samal rolled her eyes at Vovó's joke. But it turned out that there a free concert going on. Oliver and Sam weren't thrilled to be doing another activity but the harpsichord and flute performance was a relaxing way to end the day.

A Tuscan Escape

It was time to say goodbye to Rome. After a quick breakfast, the Nylund crew headed to Roma Termini, Rome's enormous train station. The twins checked out the information board displaying the timetables for all the departing and arriving trains. "Our train is delayed thirty minutes," Anara announced.

"Just enough time to visit the station's convenient store. Here are some euros, girls. Take Ollie with you."

At the shop, Ollie wanted one of those bingo boards with sliding plastic boxes on top of pictures of items you might see out the window. He also chose a word search book. Samal asked, "Isn't it weird to do word searches in a language you don't know?"

Ollie retorted, "I don't need to know Italian to find the words. You can't read the articles in that fashion magazine you're holding either."

Sam agreed, "Fair enough. I guess you're right, Ollie."

Ollie had fun with his bingo board on the ride to Tuscany. As he scoped the scenery, he checked for freight trains, olive groves, stone villas, and even swimming pools. Since Mom had meetings scheduled, she got off the train in Florence. The kids continued onto their connecting train with Vovó.

By the time they arrived at Lombardi's Tuscan Estate, it was dark outside. Dad ran up to greet them. "Hi, guys! I'm so happy you made it." He gave Vovó a hug. "Happy Birthday Mom!" Vovó had turned 65 the month before. This three-night stay in Tuscany was her belated birthday present. Anara and Samal were also excited about this leg of the trip. They were addicted to watching the Food Network, especially Italian cooking shows like "Giada at Home."

The next morning, the girls were out of bed early. Birds chirped outside and the sun streamed in through their louvered windows.

"You guys are up early," Ollie remarked.

"It's true," Samal answered. "But so is everyone else. That rooster was making a serious racket!"

The kids explored before the day's first cooking lesson. Anara dragged her sketchpad all around the place. The traditional Tuscan farmhouse was set in a working vineyard. It had a huge vegetable garden. Anara drew the morning dew on the eggplants, the myriad colors of peppers, and the view from their own little private terrace.

After his breakfast of bread and homemade apricot jam, Oliver wandered about the property. At the stables, he came across Mauricio, one of the hosts. Ollie got to brush one of the Murgesi horses bred on the farm. He loved horses. Whenever he came across a mounted police officer in Central Park back home, Oliver always asked the officer to tell him as much as possible about the horse he was riding.

Just before lunchtime, Mauricio's wife, Chiara, brought the kids out into the garden to gather ingredients for the meal they'd be preparing. Samal picked the biggest, greenest basil leaves she'd ever seen. Oliver picked some zucchini and some giant mushrooms. Anara was gathering a wicker basket full of crimson tomatoes when she let out a bloodcurdling scream. "SNAKE! Big snake! I hate snakes!" She ran as quickly as she could away from where she was standing.

Hearing the horrible shriek, Mauricio rushed over. “Una vipera! Go back to the house for now, kids, until I kill it. Chiara, get my shovel, please.” He tried to find the viper, which was slithering in the bushes.

Ollie asked, “Why does he want to kill it? I though snakes were good for keeping mice and rats away.”

“Vipers are poisonous, Oliver,” Chiara answered. “Usually they are still hibernating in February. But this warm weather must have brought the snake out.”

Anara and Sam were horrified at the idea of poisonous snakes being so close by. Anara was still shaking. She only calmed down a bit when Mauricio came back to the house, bloody shovel in hand. “It’s okay, now, girls. The snake is dead.”

The twins cautiously followed their hosts back to the garden. Chiara led the three kids over to a huge stucco structure. “Have you ever seen one of these?”

Ollie shook his head.

Samal said, “Is it an oven?”

“It sure is. And not just any oven. I call it Mauricio’s

Magic Oven because the pizzas that come out of it are like something from another world. So good! Now let's go inside and make the dough."

In the huge farmhouse kitchen, the Nylunds learned to create the perfect pizza dough. They also made pasta sauce with garlic, olive oil, and the tomatoes that Anara picked earlier in the day. Each person was in charge of assembling his or her own pizza, from crust to toppings. Mauricio helped the kids get their creations in and out of the oven.

After lunch, the kids went with Vovó on an hour-long bike ride through the Tuscan countryside. Anara loved the views of Montespertoli's rolling green hills. The ups and downs of the ride gave everyone an appetite. Luckily, they found some olives, arancini, or rice balls, and Caprese salad waiting when they returned to the farmhouse.

In the late afternoon, Oliver heard children laughing. He thought it was weird since they were the only guests at the farm. Following the sound, Ollie met up with Mauricio and Chiara's two children, Allegra and Paolo. Even though they didn't speak much English and the Nylund kids spoke no Italian,

they had fun playing hide-and-seek on the grounds.

On the second day, Oliver and Samal went on a trail ride with Mauricio. The horses were gentle, though they liked to canter on occasion. They rode along quiet trails through some nearby nature preserve land. They also passed several other tiny farms that were hidden in the hillsides.

Anara went to the local farmer's market with the grownups. But she was not happy about the dead rabbits hanging up on display. She crinkled her nose and whispered, "That is so gross, Dad. Why would anyone want to eat a cute, furry rabbit?"

Trying to be as quiet as he could, he told her, "I know you're not a big fan of eating meat, Anara, but here rabbit is practically as common as chicken. Try to look away if it bothers you. We don't want to offend Chiara." Anara helped choose citrus fruits, all kinds of local cheeses, grapes, and lots of other ingredients.

Later, Mauricio led the group in one of his favorite activities: blindfolded gelato tasting. Sam took some funny pictures of everyone wearing their checkered blindfolds, sitting around the farmhouse's huge wooden table. "You guys look ridiculous! I definitely need to email these pictures to Pari and Lola back home."

"If I look ridiculous, so do you," Anara reminded her twin. "Besides, since when is eating ice cream ever glamorous? It's always messy."

Everyone had trouble guessing what flavors of gelato and sorbet were on their spoons. Part of the problem was that the Nylunds hadn't heard of several of the fruits in their scoops, such as cachi, a member of the persimmon family, winter cherry, and black mulberry. But Oliver guessed correctly that one of his scoops was eggnog. And Samal knew pistachio. Anara said, "Hey Sam! We should totally have a blindfolded ice cream contest at our next birthday party!"

"I'm game," her sister replied.

******

The last night at Lombardi's Tuscan Estate happened to be Oliver's eighth birthday.

"What are you making, Ollie?" Samal was curious about the thick, goopy-looking batter in his mixing bowl.

“I’m making my own birthday cake,” Ollie said, his face beaming. “Chiara gave me a bunch of choices but said that her kids always asked for Nonna Stromboli’s chocolate cake on their birthdays. It’s going to be a lot of work. Want to help?”

Sam rolled up her sleeves and they spent the afternoon baking, frosting, and sampling Oliver’s fancy torta. Oliver got to choose the menu for his birthday dinner. Shortly after Mom arrived back from Florence, everyone tucked in to pasta with homemade pesto, bruschetta with tomatoes from the garden, and Oliver’s cake. Everyone learned the birthday song in Italian and serenaded Ollie with many rounds of “Tanti Auguri a te!”

Just before bed, Dad gave Oliver a gift. It was small race car. “This is a hint about something to come, Ollie. Happy Birthday and let’s race!”

Farewells and Fiery Legs

"Goodbye, Vovó! Come see us in New York soon!" Anara, Samal and Oliver waved until the car taking Vovó to the airport was out of sight.

After saying their thank-yous and goodbyes, Mauricio dropped the Nylunds off at the train station. "Is it going to take long to get where we're going, Dad?" Samal asked.

"Well, Sam, it's not a straight shot to get to Cinque Terre. But there is one stop to break up the trip."

"Where?" Ollie was curious to know.

"Little man, I'll say no more." Dad declared.

An hour later, they disembarked at the Pisa train station. A little old man sat behind a desk at the station's luggage drop-off point. Anara thought he was adorable, with his spiky white hair and glasses on a chain. He took their bags and gave them numbered plastic tags to get their suitcases back. He smiled broadly when he looked up and noticed the twins. In his best English, he said to Mom and Dad, "Two beautiful girls, one beautiful face. Che bella, how beautiful!" Both girls blushed. People in Italy seemed to get such a kick out of their wild blonde hair, pale skin, and interchangeable looks.

Ollie led the way toward the Piazza dei Miracoli, also known as the Public Square of Miracles. A brochure from the train station told Anara that some Italian poet named the square because of all its architectural gems. Sam was psyched that they were getting to see the famous Leaning Tower of Pisa. She'd seen it in some of her architecture books.

On the walk, Samal wondered aloud, "Do you guys think the pictures of the tower have been altered, like with Photoshop or something?" But her own question was answered quickly, as they approached it on foot. "Holy crow! It really is that crooked!" she marveled.

Ollie noticed the massive line to get into the tower. "Man, we're never gonna get into the tower with those lines. Didn't you guys say that we only have a couple of hours before our next train?"

"Yes, but my bosses in Florence arranged for us to have a guided tour and special pass to get in without waiting in line," Mom said.

"Wow! Fancy schmancy!" Anara giggled. "Go, Mom!"

They met up with their guide, Elena, in front of the tower. Anara was impressed with Elena's multiple ear piercings. She counted silently to herself: Eight holes in one ear and seven in the other. Anara wasn't even allowed to get one hole in her ear until she turned thirteen. Samal noticed Elena's shiny red metallic boots.

Oliver's curiosity about history meant that he had lots of questions about everything. The kids learned that the Leaning Tower was also called the Campanile, which meant bell tower. People started building it in 1173 but it wasn't actually completed until the second half of the 14th century. The reason the tower stands at such an incline is that the ground underneath it was quite soft and sunk beneath the tower's weight.

Always full of energy, Oliver led the charge up the 294 steps of the Campanile's spiral staircase. By step number 102, Anara joked, "I'm dying, you guys. I think my thighs are on fire. Seriously."

Samal quipped, "What are you, old or something? I thought you were a dancer!"

"If I'm old, you're even older," Anara replied.

"Yeah, by a whole fifteen minutes!" Samal said.

Even Ollie was winded by the time they reached the top. But the leg strain was worth it; the views of the surrounding countryside were spectacular. Back on the ground, Samal insisted that they take some selfies where they posed so it looked like they were holding up the tower.

"You guys are such goofs," Oliver told his sisters. "Are you posting these pictures online?"

"Of course," Anara laughed.

Dangers of the Sea

From Pisa, it took about two hours to get to their final destination of the day, the little village of Levanto. As soon as they arrived at their hotel, Samal sank into a cushy armchair in the living room. “I can’t move,” she said.

“Not even to walk along the beach? You might want to look out the back window before you decide to hole up for the night.” Anara and Ollie raced to the window.

“I can’t believe the ocean is right there. And the water is so blue!” Anara was impressed. The kids took an hour to relax. Then they headed down to the water for a walk on the long sandy beach.

“Last one to the water’s a rotten egg!” Ollie challenged his sisters. Even though they were older, Ollie was fast. Halfway to the shoreline, Samal stopped dead in her tracks and fell onto the sand.

"Ow! Ow! Help!" Samal's face scrunched up in pain. She had stepped on a crab while running and it was taking its revenge on her smallest toe.

Anara got to her sister first. "How do we get this thing off? It's really clamped down hard." Gingerly she poked at the crab with a stick but it wouldn't let go. Dad got there a few seconds later. He was able to push on the crab so that it released its pincers. But the damage was done. Sam's foot was pretty bloody. She was sobbing, her tears trickling down into the soft sand.

"Am I going to need stitches?" she asked. "I wish you'd killed that darn crab."

"Unfortunately, I think it's too late in the day for a doctor visit. Let's rinse the cut with saltwater and I'll bandage it up. Sorry, pumpkin." Dad soothed Samal.

The salt water stung fiercely, bringing a new round of tears to Sam's eyes. Ollie apologized to his sister for inviting her to race. "It wasn't your fault, Ollie," she told him. Even though he could drive his older sisters nuts sometimes, Oliver was a good egg. He always felt badly if someone got hurt, whether he had anything to do with it or not.

After the triage by Doctor Dad, the girls made a seashell mermaid while Ollie played catch with Mom.

A little later, the Nylund crew wandered into the town's main drag and came across a tiny seafood restaurant. Sam hobbled with one shoe on and the other off, slowly but with purpose. The salty air and sunset views of the sea were calming. All three kids chowed down on their cod and clams with minimal conversation.

Over dessert, Ollie asked about the plans for the next couple of days. Dad immediately launched into a laundry list of all the things they could do in Cinque Terre. But Anara interrupted, "Please, can we not plan just for tonight? Honestly, I'd be happy to go for a boat ride, walk around and sketch."

Dad grimaced a bit. Anara had clearly hurt his feelings. "Sure. It's just been a long time since we've been on vacation together and I want to take full advantage of it."

******

The next morning was sunny and inviting. The kids couldn't wait to head out. They kicked off the day with a beautiful three-hour hike from Levanto to

Monterosso. Oliver liked how the villages of Cinque Terre were all connected by rail, hiking paths, and boat routes. Passing by olive and lemon groves and terraced farms full of rosemary and lavender, Anara commented on the incredible smells. The pine and chestnut forests provided some shade from the bright morning sun.

One of Ollie's favorite things to do in Cinque Terre was climb the mysterious staircases. Each village seemed to have many of these, leading up the rugged cliff sides. He was thrilled to make it to the top of a staircase called Lardarina, which had 377 stairs by Sam's count – a serious workout for everyone. The mega-staircase connected Corniglia's residents with their little train station. Corniglia was a rarity in Cinque Terre because it had no direct access to the sea. This seemingly isolated town had a church dating back to 1334 called the Parish of San Pietro. Anara bought a postcard of it to send to her friend Kara.

"I hope the early architects knew what they were doing. some of Cinque Terre's colorful homes look like they could tumble into the Mediterranean Sea at any moment," Samal said.

"No kidding," Anara agreed. "I don't think I'd want to be here if an earthquake happened or even seriously heavy rains. Your house or hotel could just slip into the sea." Anara alternated between taking photos and sketching the flowers, houses, and beach umbrellas at the water's edge.

On their second day, the self-proclaimed Captain Ollie said he it was time to hit the waters. They spent the whole day ferry hopping, riding from one village to another, stopping in each one to explore a bit, browse in shops and check out the tide pools. One of the deckhands told Oliver that Cinque Terre means "five lands." He also said that when the villages were built around the 11th century, they were only accessible by footpath or boat.

On the last ferry ride, the seas seemed to be getting a bit more choppy. There was a wedding party on the boat and, Anara thought, some of them had clearly been drinking too much wine. When the boat slowed its engines to head into port, a man standing on the railing lost his balance and fell into the waters below.

The deckhands, who were focused on getting the

boat docked, didn't notice the overboard passenger right away. "Help!" a woman cried out." My fiancé is not a great swimmer." Before they knew what was happening, Dad jumped into the water. People threw them some life jackets and lifebuoy rings. Dad helped the guy get his jacket on until the crew got him back on board.

"Wow, Dad, you just saved that guy's life," Oliver was impressed. But man, you are drenched. How will you go to dinner?"

Just then, a crewmember approached Dad.

"Grazie mille," he said, handing Dad a pair of jeans and a ferry crew shirt from his own backpack.

"What'd he say?" Sam inquired.

"A thousand thank-yous," Dad told her. Finally, the ferry dropped the group off in Manarola. As soon as they stepped onto the pier, Captain Ollie declared, "Ahoy mateys, I be starving!"

They headed to a restaurant called Trattoria dal Billy that Sam came across in her research for the trip. In what might have been the longest but most delicious meal in history, the Nylunds sat around two little tables overlooking the sea. Vineyards surrounded them on three sides. They discovered blood orange soda, which fast became their new favorite beverage.

"Dad, it's pitch-black out now. Are the boats still running? Or do we have to walk back to Levanto?" She was afraid of the answer. Her foot was still quite tender when she walked on it for long periods of time.

"The boats are done for the night but there's still another train or two we could catch."

Oliver conked out before the train even pulled into Levanto station. Dad gave him a piggyback ride up the stairs to their villa. Last thing the twins heard was Mom saying, “Have fun with Dad the next couple of days. I can’t wait to see where he takes you!”

If only she had known what was to come.

Race Cars and Opera (or Hanging With Dad)

Leaving Cinque Terre, the Nylund crew split up. Mom headed to Venice for meetings. The kids went with Dad.

"Where are we going again?" Ollie asked.

Samal said, "To Modena. It has a museum that's all about sports cars like Lamborghinis and Ferraris." Sam was a bit of a fancy car expert since her Architectural Digest magazine often contained advertisements for such vehicles.

Anara rolled her eyes at Sam, but not so that Dad could see. To Samal's sense, her twin could be a bit of a diva when she didn't get her way. But Oliver shared Dad's enthusiasm for fast vehicles. "That sounds cool!" Ollie collected model sports cars. He and Dad sometimes built models of racecars on their weekends together in Brooklyn.

Anara piped in, "Did I hear you telling Mom about

going to the opera, Dad?"

"I think you should become a professional spy, Anara. I don't know when you heard that. But yes, I bought tickets online to see 'La Traviata,' my favorite opera of all time."

"Don't you have to get super dressed up to go to the opera, Dad? I didn't pack anything fancy," Samal said.

Anara thought that her sister was either a) trying to get out of having to go to the opera at all by pleading wardrobe problems or b) lobbying to get Dad to take her clothes shopping in Italy.

Mom only shopped when she had to. Like the day of a concert at school when she discovered that someone's black-and-white ensembles from the year before didn't fit anymore.

"I tell you what, Sam, let's see how the schedule works out. If we can squeak in the time, I'll try to get you a new opera-worthy ensemble. But you have to put on a good face for the other places we're going in Modena, okay? That goes for you too, Anara."

The girls nodded, looking pleased with the arrangement. After dropping their bags at the hotel, the four of them headed to the Museo Casa Enzo Ferrari. Sam loved the cool building. Its canary yellow curved roof looked like the hood of a sports car. Inside the museum, they wandered from car to car. The boys read all the specs on how fast the cars could go, how much they cost, and so on. The girls discussed which ones they'd want to drive. Anara's favorite was a Lamborghini painted hot pink with purple flames. Some rich countess had had it custom painted.

An hour later, Dad announced, "We're off to Maranello, guys. It's only about eleven miles from here."

"What are we doing there?" Anara wondered.

"Top Secret," Dad said.

As the shuttle bus pulled up in front of the Museo Ferrari Maranello, Samal read the sign and let out an audible groan. She mouthed the words "More cars?!" to Anara. But Dad shot Samal a look and reminded her that they had a deal about the car thing. Complaining meant no new clothes. So Samal quickly zipped it and put on an award-worthy smile.

Ollie and his skeptical sisters were blown away

when they got to try the F1 Simulator. For seven whole minutes, each of them felt like they were driving a Ferrari along Italy's world-famous Monza racetrack. Oliver went first and, despite his best attempts with the shifter and gearbox, had a couple of spinouts. He was whooping it up as he flew around corners. Anara turned out to be a real pro at shifting. She leaned her body into the curves as she whipped around the track. Samal was a "granny race car driver," according to Oliver. Even though she knew nothing could really happen to her in the Simulator, it was realistic enough to make her nervous. But she had fun even if she'd never be the next Mario Andretti.

After the Factory and Track tour, Dad asked, "Hey guys, I want your opinion on something. I don't know what Mom would think but there's a place near here called Push Start where adults can try out a real racecar on a track. What do you think?"

The twins were kind of blown away. Anara teased, "Are you feeling well, Dad?"

Sam asked, "Has your body been taken over by aliens? Aren't you the guy who triple-checks before every trip to make sure you've got five kinds of Band-

Aids, ointments, and sanitizer?" She grinned broadly at the thought of a wild dad.

But Oliver was thrilled by the idea. "That sounds sick, Dad! I can't wait to see you behind the wheel of some flashy race car!"

"All right, then, let's head over and see if there's any space left." As they entered the Push Start building, Oliver was so exited. Luck was on their side–there was space for Dad to race! They watched other newbies fly around the track in red, yellow, and orange Ferraris. Even the "granny driver", Samal, admitted that it was exciting to see racing up close.

During Dad's training class, one of the café workers, kept an eye on the three kids. When a race car driver entered the café wearing a black-and-white suit and a huge helmet, the kids stared. "So cool," Ollie said.

When the driver took off his helmet, they kids gasped. It was Dad! He'd finished his training course and came to the café to say he'd be racing in ten minutes–in a lime green Lamborghini Superleggera!

Samal laughed. "Isn't that the fanciest car you can race in here? Is it the one that's practically Kermit the

Frog green where the doors lift up instead of out?"

"Yep," Dad grinned. "It's amazing!"

"Go big or go home, I always say," Anara said.

Ollie, Anara, and Samal rushed out to the viewing platform to watch Dad race. They were all jumping up and down and squealing when they saw his lightning-fast car fly past them.

After Dad's circuit, the kids watched the next group of racers. "Well, how'd I do?" Dad asked when he rejoined them.

"That was SO awesome!" Anara's response mirrored what her siblings were thinking. On the ride back to the hotel, they asked a million questions about the training class, his suit and the car's control panels.

They could not believe it–Dad was a real race car driver!

******

Their second day in Modena was a little less high-octane and a little more high-fashion than the previous one. They headed to some of Modena's charming little boutiques to shop. Oliver was not excited about having to get dressed up for the opera.

He preferred to wear track pants and T-shirts every day. Shop attendants quickly outfitted him in a charcoal gray suit. They kept pinching Ollie's cheeks and telling him how handsome he looked. His sisters giggled because Ollie's face was the color of a tomato. But at least he got a cool tie with race cars on it.

The girls visited several fancy shops. Anara and Samal put on little fashion shows in each boutique. Ollie even shot some video of them doing their best supermodel impressions. Sam ended up with a purple taffeta dress for the opera and shiny patent leather shoes that were practically the same color. Anara chose a rainbow satin dress with orange leather flats. But they also got a couple of extra outfits and shoes. Dad was having a blast and enjoyed letting out his inner fashionista. The girls could not believe their good luck. Mom would never have bought them so many new clothes and shoes at once.

The evening at the Teatro Comunale Luciano Pavarotti was a memorable one. The kids didn't understand the entire story behind "La Traviata." But they were impressed with the beautiful theater, costumes, and the singers' powerful voices. But not everything was smooth. During the performance, Oliver dropped his rented opera glasses from their box seat on the second balcony. They landed with a thud on the head of a lady sitting below them. The opera came to a brief stop when the woman yelled "Yow!!" Luckily, the theater was dark so no one knew who'd dropped the glasses. They all voted to lose the deposit for the glasses and duck out at the end of the show.

Even though the show ended late, the Nylund kids went for a post-theater dessert while they were all dressed up. On the walk home, Ollie said, "Modena was really great. I liked the surprises. I can't wait to see what we're doing in Venice."

Samal agreed.

"Me, neither. I bet Venice is going to be fabulous!" Anara said.

A Not-So-Romantic Gondola Ride

After tidying their messy hotel room, each member of the Fab Four, as they jokingly called themselves on their weekends together, sipped hot chocolate on the train from Modena to Venice.

Before the last bag had even touched the platform at Venice's Ferrovia station, Oliver asked, "Can we go for a vaporetto ride? Please?"

"Isn't that basically the way everyone gets around, anyway? We can't exactly drive to our hotel, Ollie," Anara said.

Samal looked confused. "What's a vaporetto, anyway? Am I the only dodo who doesn't know?"

Dad smiled. "Of course not. A vaporetto is a canal boat used as public transit here. Since Venice has canals instead of roads, people don't use buses or trains to get around like in New York. Vaporettos are the thing. So yes, Ollie, we'll get on one now."

Standing along the edge of the boat deck, the vaporetto slowly made its way down the Grand Canal. Anara marveled at how much Venice looked like a postcard. Samal counted four brides along their relatively short ride. One stood on a bridge above her in a cream-colored gown. Two others posed with their bridesmaids in front of huge old churches. And the last stood in a balcony window in her veil, holding a bouquet of violet roses.

After dropping their bags at the Pensione dell'Orologio, Ollie asked if they could climb the Campanile since it was close by.

"More climbing?" Anara griped. "We've done so many staircases. The ones in Cinque Terre, the tower in Pisa. How different could this view possibly be?"

"Shut it, Anara. You must have taken your grumpy pill this morning. You've got your sketchpad. Just people-watch across St. Mark's Square while we're in line. Some of us want to check the bell tower out."

Even Anara had to admit that the view from the Campanile was great. It was, after all, a gorgeous day out. Oliver was convinced that he even saw some Alpine peaks in the distance. Sam thought it was neat that Galileo demonstrated his telescope from the Campanile back in 1609. She had studied Galileo last year in fourth grade.

Back at the bottom of the Campanile, Anara floated an idea by her family. “Can we just wander today? I kind of like the idea of just seeing what strikes us instead of planning. Venice has so many little alleyways and canals to check out.”

“That sounds fun,” Ollie said. “Let’s do it. We have maps.”

Sam added, “Didn’t somebody say, ‘Not all who wander are lost’? Let’s go for it.”

So for the rest of the day, the Fab Four popped into all kinds of places. They strolled through cathedrals, tiny shops that sold marbled paper, even places that made zillions of types of pasta, including black pasta, made with squid ink. No one’s requests were denied, even when Ollie insisted on going into a third candy shop.

They met up with Mom after dinner at one of the gondola ride docks. Their gondolier, Nico, was the fifth generation of his family to steer visitors along Venice’s 150-plus canals.

The ride started out pleasantly enough. Nico used his wooden pole to propel the gondola, stopping to talk about various Venetian landmarks like the Rialto Bridge and many of the palazzos, or palaces, along their route. Anara was impressed at how good Nico's English was. It was smooth sailing until Ollie let it slip that Dad raced a Lamborghini in Modena.

Ignoring the moonlit skies and beautiful surroundings, Mom went ballistic. "What would have happened if you'd crashed? Where were the kids when you were racing?" She was not quite yelling but was loud enough that other tourists they passed stared at them. The girls were completely embarrassed. Dad remained quiet.

Often wise beyond her years in such situations, Samal tried a diversion. She started asking the gondola driver tons of questions to distract everyone from the tension on board. Even Oliver figured out what Sam was up to. He asked Nico why all the gondolas were black. Nico said that back in 1562, there was a decree that said all gondolas had to be black. That way, people couldn't show off their wealth with a super-fancy looking gondola. By the end of the forty-five minute ride, the kids felt a little less uncomfortable. But it was not the nicest end to a day.

******

Everyone was calmer after a good night's rest. In the late morning the Nylunds visited a couple of mask-making shops. They needed to select masks for the UNESCO Carnival event they had tickets to. The girls struggled with whether they should choose glamorous or more fun masks. In the end, Anara chose an elephant mask since a) elephants were her favorite animals and b) she wanted to mount the mask on her bedroom wall when they returned home. Samal selected a marmalade cat mask. Oliver decided on a more traditional jester mask with brightly colored diamond shapes all over it.

After the mask shop, Oliver spent the rest of the day with Dad while Mom and the girls hung out together. It wasn't always easy to meet the interests of five people in any one outing. Oliver was thrilled to take an hour-long vaporetto ride to Burano, a neighborhood full of colorful buildings.

Anara's favorite artist in the world was Dale

Chihuly so the ladies headed to Murano, which was famous for its glassblowing and glass museum. Sam loved watching the journeymen taking the molten lumps of glass in and out of the blast furnaces and shaping little horses or vases. Before leaving Murano, the girls each got a string of brightly-colored millefiori (literally meaning "a thousand flowers") beads as a present.

When the five of them met up for dinner at a fancy Venetian restaurant, the girls wondered how the meal was going to go. While the kids were eating appetizers, something strange happened. Mom bought Dad a glass of wine at the restaurant's bar. The kids could see them but not hear anything they were saying. Anara asked her sister, "What do you think is going on? They're not having another argument, are they?"

Samal replied, "My guess? Mom's apologizing to Dad for flipping out about the Lamborghini. That was one awkward boat ride."

"No kidding." Anara agreed. "Sometimes adults are worse behaved than kids. I wanted to hide under the gondola during half the ride. Thank goodness it was dark. I'm sure my face was the color of a beet."

Oliver looked upset. "I'm sorry, I didn't know it was a secret. I wish Dad had told me not to tell Mom." The twins felt bad for Ollie. His eyes were all teary. Luckily, about fifteen minutes later, Mom and Dad returned to the table in a much better mood.

Carnival and Arrivederci (Goodbye), Italy!

"I can't believe it's our last day in Italy!" Anara moaned.

"I know, right?" Samal said. "I feel like we just arrived. There's so much more I want to see."

Oliver chose their breakfast spot, right on the Piazza San Marco. Hurried tourists scurried across the square. Strolling musicians serenaded people with their oboes and violins, hoping for a donation. The lines for the Basilica were long. Oliver was glad that he'd already gone there.

Mom threw out an idea. "One of my colleagues, Paloma, has kids in the same grades as you. When I was at my meetings the other day, she said they'd love to show you guys around their school if you're interested. She thought you could help teach English class or just see what school is like here. It's totally up to you."

Ollie wasn't too sure. He didn't love school back at home. "How long would we be there?"

"Two hours max. Paloma's kids go to Scuola Primaria, a primary school about ten minutes' walk from here. You might have fun," Mom said.

The girls said they'd like to check it out. As they were getting ready to leave the restaurant, Samal stood up from the table. "Anara, do you have my purse?"

"No, why would I have your purse? Didn't you put it on the back of your chair when we got here?" Anara replied.

"Yeah, I thought so."

Everyone looked under their jackets, inside their backpacks and under the table to see if they could find Sam's blue leather bag. After a few minutes, it was clear to them that the purse was missing.

"Was your passport in it?" Anara asked.

Sam shook her head. "Remember how when all those musicians went from café to café, a big group of people followed them. I wonder if someone stole it when I wasn't looking. But it had my ticket stubs, some money, and other little things we bought here in Venice. That totally stinks!" She was both angry and sad.

Everyone tried to boost Samal's spirits. They couldn't do much about the purse since it had no identification in it. Plus the likelihood of it being returned to the café or the police station was very low. They decided to cut their losses and head to the school.

Paloma's daughter Aurelia took the twins to her fifth grade classroom where they were wrapping up a science experiment. Anara and Samal then headed to art class where some kids were putting the finishing touches on papier-mâché masks. Then their teacher, Mrs. Caravaggio, had a question and answer session with the twins about life in America as part of their English class. The Italian students wanted to know about school buses in America, if the girls had been to the Statue of Liberty, and what their favorite foods were. Mrs. Caravaggio used Google Earth to show the class where Anara and Samal lived, went to school, and shopped for groceries.

Oliver spent time in Paloma's son's classroom. Giuseppe was a little older than Ollie, in the third grade. But his teacher, Mr. Bernini, was terrific. In the two hours Oliver was with him, Mr. B's class compared American rap music with Italian rap. Ollie was a celebrity when he rapped a few stanzas from a song called Ham 'N' Eggs. Oliver also had a great time in gym class playing Lupo Della Ore, also known as "What's The Time, Mr. Wolf?"

After their school visit, the Nylunds went out for a late lunch. Then they all went back to the hotel for a siesta.

"Mom, are you serious? I don't have to take a nap. I'm ten!" Samal griped.

"Yes, I am serious about the siesta, my friend. This UNESCO party is a really big deal and it doesn't start until 9 p.m. After you rest, we'll all prepare for the Carnival party. And Dad and I have some surprises to show you when you wake up."

Despite the complaints, Samal, Anara, and Ollie all fell asleep without any trouble. The pace of the trip had been intense since they left New York. After everyone snoozed, Mom and Dad revealed that they'd gone costume shopping while the kids were at school.

"No way! What'd you get?" The kids couldn't believe what amazing costumes they'd found to go with their new masks. Anara's elephant costume even looked like it had wrinkled skin and Samal's had the softest orange fur. Oliver's jester suit had puffy little golden bloomers with colored diamond patterns – just like on his mask.

When Ollie and his sisters walked up to the palazzo where the masked ball was being held, they couldn't believe their eyes or ears. A huge orchestra played classical music–cellos, wind instruments, even a giant harp. And all of the musicians wore masks and costumes too. Oliver thought it was hilarious that one of the flute players was dressed as a hairy gorilla. They danced with strangers and even met up with Paloma's family at the punch bowl. Aurelia and the twins had the best time making up stories in a game they called "Who's Behind That Mask?"

"Was that a fantastic end to our Italian adventures or what?" Anara exclaimed. "I thought it might be weird, especially since I can't dance. But people in Italy know how to throw a party. That was so much fun!"

The next morning, Oliver enjoyed one last boat ride in Venice–a waterbus to Marco Polo International Airport. Anara couldn't get over that that was the airport's actual name. Luckily the flight back to New York was an afternoon one. Just before they boarded their flight to New York, Mom asked, "So, Samal, you said yesterday that there was so much more you wanted to see in Italy. What did you have in mind?"

Anara, Samal, and Oliver all started rattling things off, each talking over the others. "An Inter Milan soccer game. Visiting a gelato factory. Seeing Leonardo da Vinci's home. Going to Vatican City. Hearing an Italian rap concert..."

Dad joked, "It sounds like Mom needs another work trip to Italy–and soon!"

Dear Journal,

Hello. It's Oliver Nylund here. I'm looking out our hotel window in Venice. The girls are still putting their costumes on for tonight's Carnival ball. I haven't written in here every day since we've been moving around Italy a lot. Staying at a cooking school in Tuscany was awesome! Mauricio and Chiara taught me how to make homemade pizza, pasta, even chocolate cake. I had no idea there were so many different shapes of pasta, like orecchiette, which means "little ears." Dad took a photo at a place that made pasta:

Here's Chiara's easy pesto recipe:

Ingredients
1/4 cup pine nuts or walnuts
2 cups chopped basil (packed tightly)
1/2 cup grated Parmesan cheese
2 tablespoons olive oil
2 tablespoons lemon juice
1 tablespoon water (optional)
1/2 teaspoon salt
1/4 teaspoon black pepper

Directions
Mix all ingredients in a blender or food processor until smooth. Serve over pasta, as a sauce for pizza, or on toast.

Mom had a colleague at the UNESCO office whose kids go to school here in Venice. I visited her son Giuseppe's classroom. His teacher, Mr. Bernini, wanted me to talk about my life in New York. I told the class about fun traditions like seeing the giant Christmas tree in Rockefeller Center and how we go trick-or-treating for Halloween in our apartment building. Mr. B's class told me tons of stuff I didn't know about Italy. Here's some of what I learned:

Fun Facts about Italy

Capital: Rome
Official Language: Italian
Population: 61,680,122 (July 2014 estimate)
Famous People: Marco Polo (c. 1254-1324) Leonardo da Vinci (1452-1519), Michelangelo (1475-1564); Galileo Galilei (1564-1642)
Holidays Celebrated: Republic Day (June 2); Many Italians also celebrate Christian holidays such as Easter and Christmas
Climate: mostly Mediterranean climate (hot, dry summers and mild to cool, wet winters), but varies from Alpine in the north to a hot, dry climate in the south

Significant Events

c. 800-600 BCE - Greeks and Etruscans settle in Italy
753 BCE - Rome is founded
117 CE - Roman Empire reaches its height
1298 CE - Marco Polo returns to Venice from China
c. 1300 CE - Renaissance begins
1541 - Michelangelo completes the artwork Last Judgment in the Sistine Chapel
1861 - Italy becomes a united nation, with King Victor Emmanuel II as leader
1915 - Italy enters World War I, siding with the Allies
1940 - Italy enters World War II, siding with Germany

1960 – Olympic Games held in Rome
2013 – Pope Benedict XVI resigns; Pope Francis is elected

At the beginning of the trip, I got a map of Italy that shows the boot shape of the country. Isn't it cool? Here's my copy:

I loved all the historical places we went on this trip. Visiting Rome made me feel like a time traveler. I got to see Roman ruins thousands of years old like the Colosseum. That's where Romans fought against wild animals like ostriches, deer, and even elephants! Here's a picture we took:

I was hoping to visit Ostia Antica, a busy trading center that was Rome's main port until the fifth century. My guidebook said that in Ostia you can visit a place called the Thermopolium that has a marble counter and paintings that advertise food and drink. Sounds like a Roman version of a fast-food restaurant!

If I ever come back to Italy, I also want to see Pompeii. This town was buried almost 2,000 years ago when a volcano called Mount Vesuvius erupted. It would be amazing to see what Pompeii looked like before the eruption. But no one had cameras back then!

Ruins of Pompeii

Discussion Questions

1. How is daily life in Italy today similar to life in the US? How is it different?

2. How do you think life in Italy's cities (Rome, Venice, Milan, etc.) is different from the country's more rural areas?

3. Which historical figure from Italy's past would you most like to meet and why? What would you like to ask him or her?

4. How has life in Italy changed from the days of the Roman Empire to today?

5. If you had the opportunity to visit Italy, what places or historical sites would you want to see? Why?

6. Compare Italian food to the food you eat at home in America.

Vocabulary

aria	divine	myriad
audible	enthuse	perplexing
bruschetta	fashionista	quip
cannoli	feral	ritziest
clientele	forego	sanctuary
crest	Latin	stucco
dissipate	mortified	

Ways to learn these new words

- Make flash cards with the word on one side and the definition on the other side.
- Use one of these words in a sentence.
- Draw a picture to represent the meaning of a word.
- Write a story using some of the vocabulary words.

Websites to Visit

Learn more about Italy:
www.timeforkids.com/destination/italy

Check out travel tips just for kids:
www.travelforkids.com

Learn about UNESCO's World Heritage List:
http://travel.nationalgeographic.com/travel/world-heritage/kids-family-photos/

About the Author:

From jellybeans to vampires, Alicia Klepeis loves to research fun and out-of-the-ordinary topics that make nonfiction exciting for readers. Alicia began her career at the National Geographic Society. She is the author of several kids' books, including *Africa*, *Understanding Saudi Arabia Today*, and *The World's Strangest Foods*. Her first picture book, *Francisco's Kites*, came out in May 2015. She has also written dozens of articles in magazines such as National Geographic Kids, Kiki, and FACES. Alicia is currently working on a middle-grade novel, as well as several projects involving international food, American history, and world cultures. She lives with her family in upstate New York.

About the Illustrator:

Simon Abbott has been illustrating children's books for 15 years. He specializes in bold colors and delightful characters of all kinds and describes his work as fun, fresh and happy. His easy style has instant appeal and helps to communicate complex ideas and concepts in an instant. Whether he is drawing playground fun, astronauts, dinosaurs or monkeys swinging through trees, his art is always engaging and is guaranteed to make children smile. Simon lives and works in Suffolk, England, with his partner Sally, and 3 boys called Jack, Nathan, and Alfie.